I HATE PICTURE BOOKS!

WRITTEN AND ILLUSTRATED BY
TIMOTHY YOUNG

Other Schiffer Books by the Author:

They're Coming!, 978-0-7643-4225-7, $16.99

Shadows on My Wall, 978-0-7643-4224-0, $16.99

Library of Congress Control Number: 2012953316

ISBN: 978-0-7643-4387-2
Printed in China

Published by Schiffer Publishing, Ltd.
4880 Lower Valley Road
Atglen, PA 19310
Phone: (610) 593-1777; Fax: (610) 593-2002
E-mail: Info@schifferbooks.com

For the largest selection of fine books, like this one, please visit our website at
www.schifferbooks.com. You may also write for a free catalog.

This book may be purchased from the publisher.
Please try your bookstore first.

We are always looking for people to write books on new and related subjects. If you have an idea for a book, please contact us at
proposals@schifferbooks.com

Schiffer books are available at special discounts for bulk purchases for sales promotions or premiums. Special editions, including personalized covers, corporate imprints, and excerpts can be created in large quantities for special needs. For more information, contact the publisher.

I HATE PICTURE BOOKS!

WRITTEN AND ILLUSTRATED BY
TIMOTHY YOUNG

Dedicated to my Mom, who filled my childhood with picture books,
and to Rosemary Morris, the best, most-helpful children's
librarian I know.

BUT WHEN I DREW ON THE WALL,
SHE SENT ME TO BED
WITHOUT DINNER!

I was very ANGRY so I wished my room would turn into a forest and then a boat would come take me away. The next morning I woke up to find...

NOTHING!
NO FOREST!
NO BOAT!
NO WILD THINGS ANYWHERE!
NOTHING BUT MY STUPID ROOM AND MY STUPID PICTURE BOOKS!

I started to think that I really didn't like picture books at all!

I MEAN, THEY'RE REALLY DUMB...

Because Toy Bears don't talk or walk around...

and Cow's Can't Type...

I'D LIKE TO SEE THEM PUT
THAT IN A PICTURE BOOK!

But the worst thing, there's this book about this baby bird.

It can't find its mother and it looks everywhere.

None of these animals can help the baby bird.

So you know what *this book* made me do?

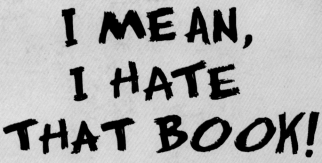

I MEAN,
I HATE
THAT BOOK!

IT WAS THE FIRST
ONE I THREW AWAY.

Wait...
I DO love that book.

I can't throw away any of these. I mean, I love this book about the flying snowman...

and the one with the great, big stack of turtles...

and this one with the mouse who wants a cookie...

or this one where the bears hunt for honey!

I don't know what I was thinking,
I can't throw away all these books!